Tiberius
and the Rainy Day

Keith Harvey

Illustrated by Paula Hickman

Award Publications Limited

ISBN 978-1-84135-920-5

Written by Keith Harvey
Illustrated by Paula Hickman

First published by Tiberius Publishing Limited

This edition first published by Award Publications Limited 2013

Published by Award Publications Limited,
The Old Riding School, The Welbeck Estate,
Worksop, Nottinghamshire, S80 3LR

www.awardpublications.co.uk

13 1

Printed in China

Drag's Cave

Fitzwarren
Castle

N
W E
S

Signpost

Sneaky's
House

The Park

Cringleford
Down

Torpedo's
Place

To Widdecombe Park

Tiberius's
House

Croaky's
Tree

Winchester
Towers

The Woods
(where Sebastian Squirrel lives)

Jumble
Farm

Gordon's
House

To Puddledock Green

Witchford

It had been raining all night. Tiberius woke up early. He had so many things to do, but when he looked out of the window it was still raining.

"What shall I do?" said Tiberius, looking at the rain as it came pouring down, forming big puddles on his path.

"It's raining so heavily, I don't really want to go out."
Tiberius went to the door and opened it. The raindrops were beating on the door so hard that they came into the house.
"It's no good," he said to himself, shutting the door. "I will just have to stay inside until it stops."

Just then, the phone rang. It was Mrs Cake from the cake shop in the village. "Hello, Tiberius," said Mrs Cake, "I wonder if you could help me?"

"I'm sure I can," said Tiberius, "providing it doesn't involve going outside. It's raining so hard."

"That's the trouble," said Mrs Cake, "I'm stranded in my shop. There is water all the way up to the front door and it seems to be rising every minute. The shop is soon going to be full of water."

"Oh dear," said Tiberius, "I'm sure we can do something."

Tiberius scratched his head and looked out of the window.
If he went outside, he felt he could be swept away by the rain.
The puddles on his path were growing bigger and bigger.
"Don't worry, Mrs Cake," said Tiberius, "I will ring Drag and
we will come round and rescue you."

"Thank you so much," said Mrs Cake.

'What should I do first?'
thought Tiberius, as he slowly
put down his phone. 'I know, I
shall ring Drag, he will help.'
Drag's phone rang and
rang and rang, but there was
no reply. 'Oh dear, I'll have
to try Croaky Crow.' He rang
Croaky and his phone rang
and rang and rang.

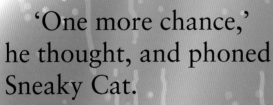

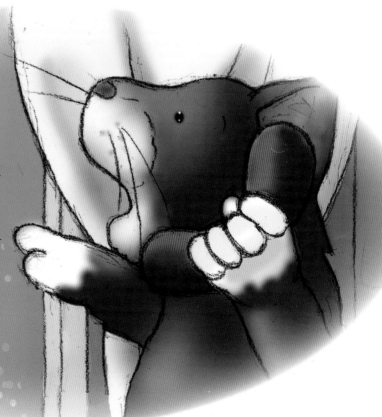

'One more chance,'
he thought, and phoned
Sneaky Cat.
Sneaky Cat answered
straight away, "Hello!
Sneaky Cat here."

"Hello, Sneaky," said Tiberius, "I have a problem, but I don't think I will be able to get out of the door as it's raining heavily and there are big puddles all the way to the gate."

"It's raining here too," said Sneaky, "but what is the problem?"

Tiberius told Sneaky about Mrs Cake's phone call.

"Don't worry," said Sneaky. "I don't like rain very much, but this is urgent. I will be with you in ten minutes."

When Sneaky reached Tiberius's house, he stopped at the gate. Tiberius waved to him from the door.

"I don't think you will get through the water!" Tiberius shouted to him.

"I won't," said Sneaky, "but I know someone who can."

"So do I," called Tiberius. "Where do you think he will be?"

"Asleep as usual," said Sneaky Cat, "all warm and cosy in his cave. I will go and find him now."

With that, Sneaky Cat ran off down the road, splashing through the puddles. He ran up the hill to Drag's cave.

When he arrived at the cave's entrance, he called, "Drag, Drag!" A very sleepy voice from inside said, "Hello, who is that? It's so very cold and wet this morning, won't you just let me sleep?"

"It's me," said Sneaky Cat. "You've got to get up. Tiberius needs you, and so does Mrs Cake!"

Drag sat up and rubbed his eyes.

"Tiberius needs you to help him out of his house, and then we have to go to Mrs Cake's."

Drag found his wellies and
the biggest umbrella you have
ever seen. It was almost like
a tent without any sides!
   "I'm ready," said
Drag with a smile
on his face.
"Let's go!"

   "You are going to
enjoy this, Drag," said
Sneaky Cat.
   "Of course," said Drag,
"this doesn't happen every day!"

When they arrived at Tiberius's house, Drag left Sneaky Cat
at the gate and waded through the water.

The rain was beating down loudly on his umbrella.

"Oh, Drag," said Tiberius as he opened the door, "I'm so
pleased to see you."

"Are you ready?" asked Drag.
"Yes! We must hurry and
rescue Mrs Cake," said Tiberius.
"It's urgent!"
    "Hop on, then," said Drag.

With that, Tiberius hopped
onto Drag's arm, and then
onto his shoulder, and
then onto his head. Tiberius
looked up at the inside of the
umbrella. 'It's lovely and dry
under here,' he thought.

When they reached the gate, Sneaky Cat shot under the umbrella. "I was getting really soaked standing here," he said. "You know how I don't like water."

Drag and Tiberius laughed.

"You don't like heights, either," said Tiberius.

At that moment Croaky Crow came flying down out of the sky.

"Hello, you three!" he said. "Where are you going to in this awful weather?"

Tiberius explained that they were off to rescue Mrs Cake, as her shop was surrounded by water.

"We'd better hurry, then!" said Croaky.

Off they went. *Splish, splash, splish, splash.*

It wasn't long before they saw Mrs Cake's shop in the distance.
Streams of water were rushing down the side of the road.
"I hope she's alright," said Drag.
"So do I," said Tiberius.
It was then that Croaky spotted something in the water.

"Look, what's that?"
he said. "And look, there's
another, and another."

Floating down the road were three
of Mrs Cake's fancy cupcakes.
"Oh dear," said Tiberius. "She must
be in trouble if the cakes are sailing
down the road!"

Sure enough, when they arrived at the shop, Mrs Cake was standing at the open window, throwing more cakes into the water.

"Oh, thank goodness you have come," she said. "I thought nobody would know I was stranded. I didn't know what to do, as my phone is now out of order. I thought if I threw out enough cupcakes someone might recognise them as a distress signal."

The four friends couldn't help smiling. "It was a good idea," said Croaky, "but you should have known Tiberius wouldn't let you down."

The water had almost reached up to the doorstep.

"What shall we do?" Mrs Cake called out to Tiberius.

"I think we will be all right," shouted Tiberius.
"The rain seems to be stopping." Drag carried the three
friends to the shop door and Mrs Cake let them in.

"Oh, I'm so pleased to see you," she said. Fortunately the water hadn't leaked into the shop.

"The water is going down now," said Tiberius,

"What a relief!" said Mrs Cake. "But what will I do if it rains like this again?"

"You need to fetch some sacks and fill them with sand and stack them up in the doorway," said Croaky.

"Will that really help?" asked Mrs Cake, doubtfully.

"Oh yes," Tiberius assured her. "Haven't you seen the pictures on the TV when there's a flood? There are always sandbags piled up in doorways to stop water coming into houses."

"Well, I will certainly make sure I'm prepared for next time!" answered Mrs Cake.

"Don't worry," said Drag, "we'll always be here to help!"

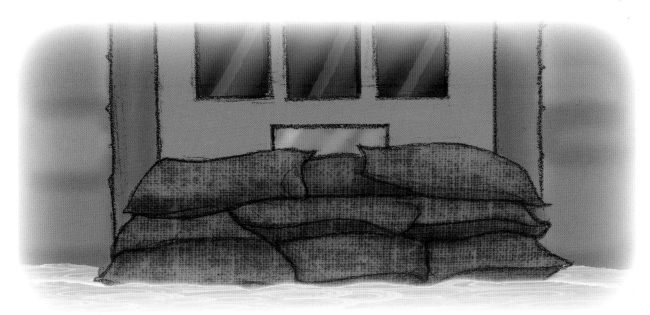

Mrs Cake then brought out a big plate of cakes and some drinks for Tiberius and his friends. They all sat around the table.

"What an exciting rainy day we've had," said Tiberius. "We're so pleased we could help you, Mrs Cake."

"I'm so glad you did!" she said. "What would have happened to all my cakes without you?"

"Never mind that," said Croaky. "Can you imagine the village without Mrs Cake's special chocolate cake and cupcakes!"

Everyone smiled as they tucked into the feast.